Pirate's Treasure

by Marcy Kelman

illustrated by Andy Mastrocinque

Based on the episode written by Claudia Silver and Jeff Borkin

Disney PRESS

New York

The Little Einsteins were playing dress-up in the Rocket Room.

"Ahoy, there, me hearties," Quincy said in his best pirate voice. "I spy a treasure map over yonder."

"Yo-ho-ho!" shouted Annie. "A treasure map could mean only one thing."

June carefully studied the ancient scroll. "Hmm, according to this map, we need to steer around four buoys, sail over a huge wave, and then do some island hopping to get to the buried treasure." Annie was puzzled. "How do you know where to find the buried treasure?"

"Because 'X' always marks the spot," answered Quincy. *Can you find the "X" on this treasure map?*

The team followed the treasure map, sailing around all four buoys, but they ran into trouble once they reached the big wave.

"Blimey!" scowled Quincy. "What is Big Jet doing here?"

"ARGGH!" groaned June. "Big Jet is the least of our worries—the treasure map just fell overboard!"

"Quick, Rocket, go into submarine mode," Captain Leo commanded.

Underwater, the team soon learned that they had to complete a scavenger hunt before going after the map.
Can you help them find six orange fish, five sea stars, four sea turtles, three sea horses, two crabs, a jellyfish, and a lobster?

After the scavenger hunt, a friendly dolphin appeared.

"The dolphin keeps swimming around Rocket—I think he's trying to tell us something!" said Annie.

"Maybe he knows where the map is," suggested Leo. "Let's use Rocket's Look-and-Listen Scope to pick up the sounds he's making."

Rocket picked up the dolphin's secret message on the Look-and-Listen Scope, but it looks as though some letters are missing. Using the letters A, E, I, O, and U, can you help decode the message the dolphin is sending to the team?

TH_ M_P _S _N

TH_ S_NK_N SH_P

"Looks like we're not the only ones who figured out Dolphin's message—Big Jet is headed straight for the sunken ship," cried Leo.

"That scallywag—we've got to get to the map before he does!" bellowed Quincy.

Who will get the map first? Lift the flap to find out!

June has a plan to get the map back. Will you help her carry it out? Great! First, flap your arms and pretend you're a fish swishing through the water. Next, scrunch up your lips as though you are about to give a kiss and then—SMACK!—make very loud smooching noises!

"Great job, everybody!" June exclaimed. "You're all doing the kissing-fish dance!"

It worked! The dance attracted a school of kissing fish, and they're all busy distracting Big Jet with a flurry of kisses.

Will the kisses be enough to make Big Jet lose his grip on the map? Find out by lifting the flap!

"We're getting closer to the buried treasure," said Annie. "We just need to hop over a few islands."

"Okay, Rocket, it's time to use your Pogo Bouncer," ordered Captain Leo.

"Let's hop to it!" said Quincy. "Land ho!"

How many hops will it take to get to the buried treasure?

Look, the team found the spot! Let's celebrate by singing with Annie:

YO, HO, HO!
Let's do a pirate jig.
Where "X" marks the spot,
For treasure we will dig!

YO, HO, HO!
There is no time to rest
When pirates are in search
Of a buried treasure chest!

Rocket used his Super Scooper to dig where "X" marked the spot, and he uncovered the buried treasure chest!
Leo beamed with pride as Rocket retrieved the chest. "I knew you could do it, Rocket!"

What do you think is inside the chest? Open it up and find out!

It was an old nautical whistle. "**TOOOOOT! TOOOOT!**"
blew Quincy.

When Quincy stopped blowing the whistle, something magical
appeared in the sky.

"A rainbow–how marvelous, " gasped June.

"Well, shiver me timbers," laughed Leo. "Now that's what I call a
colorful adventure!"

"**Mission completion!**" said Leo.